Where I Come From

Clare McBride

Illustrated by:
Bonnie Lemaire

Where I Come From
Copyright © 2021 by Clare McBride

All rights reserved. No part of this publication may be reproduced, distributed, or transmitted in any form or by any means, including photocopying, recording, or other electronic or mechanical methods, without the prior written permission of the author, except in the case of brief quotations embodied in critical reviews and certain other non-commercial uses permitted by copyright law.

Tellwell Talent
www.tellwell.ca

ISBN
978-0-2288-5155-4 (Hardcover)
978-0-2288-5154-7 (Paperback)

In loving memory of Oksana and Quinn,
my beautiful blue-eyed prairie girls,
who found fun wherever they went.

#forever6and4 #dontdrinkanddrive

www.claremcbride.com

Where I come from,

we grow our own food – potatoes, carrots, and peas – to share with our neighbours.

Where I come from,

it gets so hot I feel as if I'm melting, like a sticky, purple popsicle.

Where I come from,

it gets so cold I feel as if I'm turning into a cool, chubby snowman.

Where I come from

is a busy little, prairie town,
where the seasons are always changing,
but my heart is always warm.

Where I come from,
is the Parkland of Manitoba.

Where do you come from?

About the Author

The oldest of three girls, Clare McBride was born in Northern Ireland. At age nine, Clare immigrated with her family to Canada, where she spent the rest of her childhood on a prairie grain farm. Since college, Clare has worked in the agricultural industry. Author of *Pearl Loves Her Name*, she writes to honour the memory of her two daughters, Oksana and Quinn.

Manufactured by Amazon.ca
Acheson, AB